NEVER MAIL AN ELEPHANT

BY
MIKE THALER
ILLUSTRATED BY
JERRY SMATH

WHISTLESTOP ®

Troll Associates

For all the wonderful gang
at the Stone Ridge Post Office, 12484.
M.T.

For the hard-working people at the
Croton-on-Hudson Post Office, 10520.
J.S.

Library of Congress Cataloging-in-Publication Data

Thaler, Mike, (date)
Never mail an elephant / by Mike Thaler; pictures by Jerry Smath.
p.   cm.
''A Laffalong book''—T.p. verso.
Summary: The narrator has trouble mailing an elephant as a
birthday present to Cousin Dilly.
ISBN 0-8167-3018-0 (lib. bdg.)   ISBN 0-8167-3019-9 (pbk.)
[1. Birthdays—Fiction. 2. Elephants—Fiction.] I. Smath,
Jerry, ill. II. Title.
PZ7.T3Ne 1994
[E]—dc20   93-14395

Text copyright © 1994 by Mike Thaler.

Illustrations copyright © 1994 by Jerry Smath.

Published by Troll Associates, Inc.
WhistleStop is a trademark of Troll Associates.

Printed in the United States of America.

10 9 8 7 6 5 4

One day I decided to mail my cousin Dilly
an elephant for her birthday.

So I went to the stationery store
and got lots of wrapping paper.

Then I went to the hardware store
and got a big ball of string.

Next I emptied my piggy bank and went
to the post office to get lots of stamps.

Then I went to the zoo and got an elephant.

I covered the elephant with wrapping paper,

wound it round with string, and tied a bow.

Then I addressed it.
The elephant giggled because it tickled.

I let my dog Lucky lick the stamps.

Then I pasted them on.

Lucky's tongue stuck to the floor.
I pulled him loose.

Then we put the elephant on my wagon...

and pulled it to the corner mailbox.

Then I pushed...and shoved...

and stuffed the elephant in!

As I headed for home I met the mailman

and told him about the elephant.

The mailman went to the mailbox
and opened the door.

Then he pulled...and tugged...

...and yanked the elephant out!

Then he wrestled it onto his cart

and putted slowly to the post office.

The postmaster put the elephant on the scale.
Then he stamped it!

The elephant went WILD!
Its legs shot out of the wrapping paper.

It jumped into the air, crashed through the wall...

...and ran all the way back to my house.
Since Dilly's birthday was that afternoon,
I did the next best thing I could do...

I tied a pink ribbon around the elephant.

Then Lucky and I climbed on top

and rode it next door to her party.

Happy birthday!